GLADIATOR BOY

ESCAPE FROM EVIL

Other Gladiator Boy titles to collect:

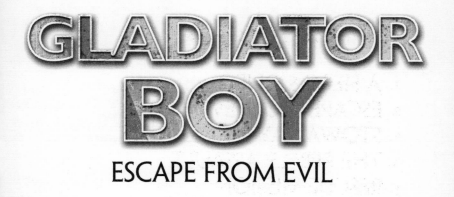

GLADIATOR BOY

ESCAPE FROM EVIL

DAVID GRIMSTONE

*Hodder
Children's
Books*

A division of Hachette Children's Books

Text copyright © 2009 David Grimstone
Illustration copyright © 2009 James de la Rue

First published in Great Britain in 2009
by Hodder Children's Books

The rights of David Grimstone to be identified as the author
and James de la Rue to be identified as the illustrator of the Work have been
asserted by them in accordance with the Copyright, Designs and Patents Act 1988.

4

A Catalogue record for this book is available from
the British Library

ISBN: 978 0 340 97052 2

Typeset by Tony Fleetwood

Printed and bound in Great Britain by CPI Bookmarque, Croydon

The paper and board used in this paperback by Hodder Children's Books are
natural recyclable products made from wood grown in
sustainable forests. The manufacturing processes conform to the
environmental regulations of the country of origin.

Hodder Children's Books
a division of Hachette Children's Books
338 Euston Road, London NW1 3BH
An Hachette UK company

www.hachette.co.uk

*For Olive Tripodi, mother-in-law
and creator of teddy-bears!*

I would like to dedicate the entire Gladiator Boy *series
to* Terry Pratchett. *There is no writer, living or dead,
for whom I have greater respect. Thank you
for everything.*

CONTENTS

ANCIENT ITALY

PREVIOUSLY IN GLADIATOR BOY

Captured by slave-takers, Decimus Rex is forced to endure a series of trials in the dreaded Arena of Doom. With his five cellmates, Decimus faces a race over burning hot coals. He is then forced into violent hand-to-hand combat with a fellow slave. Life can't get any more difficult than this – or can it?

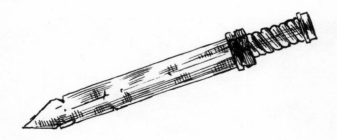

CHAPTER I

THE GREAT FALL

Decimus closed his eyes.
Surrounded by a ring of spikes,
he was fighting for his life
against a fellow slave. He wasn't sure he was
going to make it. Locked in a powerful choke
hold and lifted from the ground, Decimus
found himself rushed towards the edge of the
combat circle in the mammoth hands of
Boma Derok.

Screaming with rage, Decimus shifted his
weight several times to no avail – the big
slave was so strong that it was like trying to
struggle against a moving boulder.

The two combatants had nearly reached
the spikes when Decimus suddenly snaked
down a hand and raked his fingernails across
Boma's eyes. The big slave dropped his

opponent immediately, and raised both hands to his scratched face.

Decimus landed on his feet, hopped around behind the wounded fighter and threw all his weight at him. Boma staggered forward, palms still covering his eyes, and tripped on the line of spikes. He was doomed.

As the fickle slave crowd roared its approval, Boma Derok plunged face-first into the sand.

The combat was over.

Decimus wasn't quite prepared for the admiration and cheers he received that night in the cell section. Gladius couldn't stop talking about the fight, Olu and Ruma both offered Decimus their own soup and even Argon reached through the bars and shook his hand. Further down the corridor, whispers and distant shouts could be heard: the name Decimus was spreading along the corridors like wildfire. Boma Derok's fate would now be a subject few discussed, his name forgotten by all but his cellmate and presumably – in some distant town – by his family. Meanwhile, he would rot in the underground prisons.

Decimus knew he could easily have suffered the same destiny and, to Gladius's surprise, decided to scratch the big slave's name into the cell floor with his spoon. Boma didn't deserve to be forgotten: no one did.

'There's something going on out there.'

At first, Decimus thought the words had been spoken by Gladius, but his friend was staring past him. Turning, he saw that his eyes were on Ruma, who had squeezed himself against the barred door of his cell and was straining to see down the far end of the corridor. Behind him, Olu had drifted off to sleep.

'What's up?' said Argon, getting to his feet

and heading across to the front of his own cell.

'Whispers,' said Ruma, holding up a hand in order to keep the others quiet. 'Apparently, there's a lot of noise coming from the arena.'

'Fighting?' Decimus asked, sharing a hopeful glance with Gladius.

Ruma shook his head. 'No, more like building; you know, hammering and work noise.'

Argon was now pressed against the barred door separating his cell from the corridor. 'What's that?' he said.

'Just wait,' snapped Ruma, as Olu began to stir. 'I can't hear anything with you talk—'

'No, not the noise – what is that?'

Ruma tried to follow Argon's pointing finger and squinted into the shadows. 'I don't know what you're looking at!'

'On the wall! Just up the corridor!' Argon sneaked a hand through the bars and extended his finger as far as it would reach. 'THERE!'

Ruma squinted harder. 'Keys,' he said, eventually. 'It's a hook – Truli keeps his ring of cell keys on it.'

'Can you get to it?' Gladius hazarded.

Ruma laughed. 'Are you crazy? Do you think I have ropes for arms or something?'

They all burst into fits of laughter ... but Decimus said nothing. He was staring very thoughtfully into the shadows.

When the slave horde arrived in the arena the following morning, Master Falni had taken control of the trials. From what Decimus could tell, this wasn't good news: a series of giant poles had been erected, each supporting a circular wooden platform at its summit.

'They get smaller and smaller,' said Ruma, his sharp eyes taking in the scene before him. 'And they also get further apart.'

Decimus nodded. He had spotted a ladder next to the distant pole supporting the largest platform. It didn't take a genius to work out what was expected of the slaves.

'I notice Slavious Doom never watches any of the trials,' Olu whispered. He spoke so rarely that his voice caused everyone to turn towards him. 'At least, if he is watching I haven't seen him.'

'No,' Decimus agreed. 'He hasn't been here. I'm thinking he probably won't show up until the end of the trials.'

'Ha!' Argon exclaimed. 'Then the chances are none of us will ever see him.'

'Decimus might,' said Gladius, without a trace of humour in his voice.

'Yeah,' admitted Ruma, smiling. 'Decimus might.'

A piercing cry shook the group from their huddled conversation. Master Falni was calling for silence.

'This trial will test your agility to its very limits. In the next few minutes, I will ask you all to line up beside the ladder at the bottom of the far pole. Once assembled, each of you will climb the ladder and try to make it across the eight platforms that stand between the first and last poles. When the first boy reaches the finishing platform – or falls during the effort – the next boy may begin. Once you have completed the course, you will rejoin the queue in order to go again. Our servants will ensure that no one escapes the line or tries in any way to drop back. ALL will be tested.'

Falni took a few moments to let the rules of the trial sink in before he added: 'The contest will end when seventeen boys have fallen and only thirty-two remain.'

This time, several gasps rose up from the gathered slaves. Decimus and Gladius shared horrified glances with Olu, Argon and Ruma.

'Seventeen of us!' Argon spluttered. 'That isn't a trial – it's slaughter!'

'I don't stand a chance,' Gladius muttered. He turned to Decimus, and whispered in his ear. 'Don't suppose you have any good tips for this one?'

Decimus shrugged. 'Don't fall?'

'Ha! I'd worked that one out for myself, thanks.'

'I still don't really understand all this,' Argon confessed, aloud. 'How can he earn back the money our families owe if most of us end up in his stinking prison?'

'It's simple,' said Ruma. 'He only needs one decent champion to attract a major crowd . . . and, let's face it, anyone who survives this lot is bound to make a decent champion. He'll probably make more Denarii from one event than the amount all our families owe him put together.'

'Shhh!' Gladius interrupted. 'We're meant to be lining up.'

Forty-nine slaves queued at the bottom of the first pole, watching as the first of their number began to climb the long ladder that

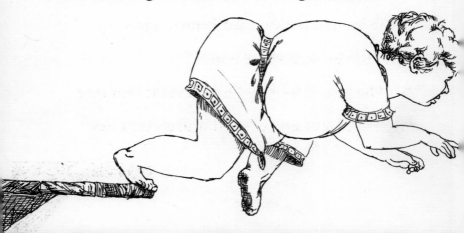

led to the platform above. He was a boy
Decimus hadn't seen before: slow, ponderous
and even larger than Gladius. He was almost
totally out of breath by the time he reached
the platform, but was quickly spurred into
action by the impatient roar of the ageing
trial-master.

Decimus wanted to look away, but he
found his gaze rooted to the slave, who took
a running leap . . .

. . . and fell before he reached the
second platform.

Gladius gulped.

'He landed badly,' said Ruma. 'He's
probably broken some bones.'

The group looked on as several servants
lifted the slave and carried him away. They

could still hear the boy's sobs of distress when he was halfway to the portcullis.

'This is bad,' said Argon, as the next slave began to climb towards his fate. 'This is really bad.'

The new boy, who was considerably smaller than the first, reached the first platform and didn't even pause before beginning his run-up. He landed evenly on the second platform, receiving an unexpected whoop of cheers in the process. He leapt across to the next stage with equal skill, taking some time to catch his breath while his fellow slaves looked on.

Decimus watched, silently praying for the boy while at the same time having to admit he would stand a better chance of getting through the round if he fell.

Fourth platform – no problem. Fifth, sixth. It was looking good. Then, suddenly . . .

Decimus knew the boy hadn't taken enough of a run-up for the jump needed to attain the seventh platform. The gap was big for someone with such short limbs, and he just knew – deep down – that the boy's jump would see him fall short. He was right.

The boy plummeted to the ground, and was quickly dragged away by the servants. The trial continued. Decimus shuffled along the line, Gladius behind him and Olu, Argon and Ruma in front. He wondered which of their small group would return to the cells that night . . .

By the time Olu stood next to the ladder,

twelve slaves had fallen victim to the evils of the trial. Decimus found himself shaking with fear as Olu quickly climbed to the first platform.

Rather than watch the quiet boy leap between each platform, Decimus chose instead to look down at the sand, relying on the gasps and sighs of the other slaves to inform him of Olu's progress. Fortunately, there were a lot of gasps . . . but not a single sigh.

Olu completed the course with a heart-stopping leap from the seventh platform. Despite missing the eighth platform, he managed to catch hold of the edge and drag himself to victory. A roar went up from the slaves, and Olu returned to the end of the queue.

Argon's own trial got off to a speedy start, and the Gaul only encountered a problem between platforms seven and eight, tripping as he landed and almost toppling over the edge. Luckily, he managed to save himself . . . and Decimus heaved a sigh of relief.

Ruma gave everyone an early scare when he missed the second platform and ended up clinging on to the wooden fringe like a man trying to stop himself falling from the edge of a steep cliff. Once he'd pulled himself up, however, the rest of his jumps were completed with comparative ease.

Decimus took a deep breath, looked up at the platform and began to climb.

'Good luck,' Gladius whispered. 'Remember – don't look down!'

His heart thumping in his chest, Decimus hauled himself on to the platform, paused briefly to take another breath, and sprinted up to the edge.

Leap.

The thing that shocked Decimus, when he landed safely on the other side, was just how unstable the platforms were. For a moment, he felt the wooden stage tilt beneath him and actually thought it might collapse. Then he found his footing ... and the third platform loomed. He jumped it without a second's hesitation, and only took a moment to steel himself when he landed on the fourth.

Platforms five and six also passed without disaster, and Decimus finally found himself preparing for the jump that had claimed so many slaves before him.

He took a final gulp of air.

One . . .

Two . . .

Three . . . leap.

CRASH.

Decimus landed on the eighth platform with such force that he actually pitched forward and almost toppled over the opposite edge. Fortunately, his legs buckled beneath him and he crumpled on to the wooden stage, accompanied by a roar of approval from the crowd.

As he climbed down and joined the slave line behind Ruma, Decimus saw that Gladius was about to take the trial. He couldn't watch.

Turning his eyes to the sand once again, he almost wished he could block out all sound, as well. Gasps and sighs had accompanied the endeavours of just about every slave who had taken the trials ... and Gladius's own jumps were no different.

Decimus watched the sand, hearing three sets of shocked gasps ... and one very audible sigh.

He looked up, sharp. Gladius had missed the fourth platform and was hanging from it, trying to haul his immense bulk over the edge with every ounce of strength he had in him.

Decimus closed his eyes and prayed for the

gods to give his cellmate the power to save himself. When he opened them again, Gladius was sprawled on the sand . . . and the arena servants were already gathering round him.

Decimus clenched his fists and muttered a curse. The gods had ignored him, and now his friend would be thrown into some dark and foul-smelling prison in order to serve out his family's crime. It wasn't fair. Life wasn't fair.

The line moved on. Gladius became the course's thirteenth victim, but it would

require more failures before the trial-master's thirst for prisoners would be quenched.

Fortunately for Decimus and his remaining companions, four boys had fallen before any of them reached the ladder for a second run.

The trial was over.

CHAPTER
II

CLASH
OF THE
HAMMERS

A sombre night in the cells gave way to a morning that, for Decimus, passed in a complete haze. Argon and Ruma had both tried and failed to cheer him up. Even Olu had offered a few rare words of condolence.

After breakfast, the group walked out to their new trial like a pack of trained zombies. No conversation passed between them, and Decimus almost felt as though his limbs were being controlled by the gods: his legs felt heavy and his arms swung loosely at his sides. As they entered the arena for their fourth trial, he found himself missing Gladius's whining voice: glancing around him, he suspected that Argon, Ruma and Olu were missing it, too.

The slave line marched on to the hot sand, and was greeted with a sight that filled each and every boy with absolute terror. A row of what could only be described as *giants* stood before them. The men were all over seven feet tall and bare-chested, with bulging muscles and hands like great slabs of meat. They each wore tattered loin-cloths and every one carried a vast, long-handled hammer.

The three trial-masters stepped forward, but it was only Mori who spoke.

'Today is the day when thirty-two slaves will be reduced to sixteen!' he cried. 'Behold, The Trial of the Hammer!'

A gong sounded, and the entire slave line turned to face the direction of the sound. Decimus noticed that Mori, Hrin and Falni had all lowered their heads.

Behind the gong, which had been brought

out by the servants and positioned atop one of the lower stalls, was an arched doorway. Decimus had seen it many times during the trials, but he had never seen anyone walk through it . . . until now.

A collective intake of breath accompanied the arrival of two of the most distinctive figures Decimus had ever seen in his life. The first was a tall, dark warrior in a suit of golden armour. A dark face and beard were visible beneath a helmet crested with two winged demons bowed in submission. Beside the first man was a figure wreathed in shadow: a dark cloak with an overflowing hood that betrayed not a hint of flesh. The armoured figure took a seat on the nearest bench, its mysterious companion moving to stand behind it.

'You are indeed honoured today, boys,' trial-master Mori continued. 'Your trial today will be witnessed by Grand Master Slavious Doom and the legendary Drin Hain.'

Decimus leaned toward Ruma. 'Which one is Doom?' he whispered.

Ruma shrugged, a confused expression on his face. It was Argon who spoke.

'Doom is the warrior with the demon-helm,' he said. 'Legend says he took it from an underground tomb. The other one must be Hain, but I've never heard of . . .'

'They call him the Wrath of Doom,' said Olu suddenly, prompting the usual surprised reaction from his fellow slaves. 'He is an assistant to Slavious; a slave-taker. There are rumours that he once tracked an escaped slave to the edge of the world, and beyond . . .'

Olu stopped speaking, but Argon, Decimus and Ruma had already returned their attention back to the demonic pair in the stalls. However, Mori's continued roar shook them from their reverie.

'On the sand before you are thirty-two golden shields. Your task during this trial is simple: take up a shield and form a line opposite these formidable gladiators. You will then need to stand your ground against the onslaught of the hammer. Those who fall will be eliminated from the trials; those who remain standing will go through to our last sixteen.'

Mori turned and bowed to Slavious Doom, and the contest was underway.

Decimus wasted no time. He raced forward and snatched up a shield, staggering slightly under the immense weight of the thing: he'd expected it to be heavy, but not quite this heavy. It was huge, too – when he held it against his chest, the circular plate just about covered his entire torso: there was barely enough room to see over the top.

Beside him, Argon had snatched up his own shield, while Ruma and Olu (who were both considerably weaker) struggled to even lift theirs.

'Chaaaaaaaaaarge!'

The scream had erupted from Mori, who dropped his hand in a signal mere seconds before the incredible line of giants tore forward in a determined rush.

Decimus waited with bated breath. Suddenly, there was a monstrous crash, and a slave three positions away from him flew back as though he had been fired from a cannon. The boy's shield clattered to the ground . . .

SLAM!

Decimus felt the blow drive him back. His heels threw up several sprays of sand as he quickly flattened his feet and tried to maintain his balance. He dropped the shield but didn't let go, allowing the edge of the plate to dig into the ground in an effort to halt his backward progress: it worked, and he slowed to a stop. Looking out, he saw that most of the slaves on his right were down: only Argon still stood behind his shield, his face contorted with determined rage.

Decimus caught his breath and glanced to his other side. Incredibly, Olu and Ruma were also still on their feet, though Ruma's shield must have glanced off his head, as a nasty cut had opened above his right eye. Beyond the pair, a further three slaves had gone down. Decimus tried to total the number of those who had fallen in his head, but Mori's voice rang out before he could complete the count.

'Only nine have fallen!' he boomed, as the servants swarmed on to the sand to retrieve the prone unfortunates. 'Therefore, there will be a second round. Take up the shields and prepare yourselves!'

This time, Decimus had a few moments to think as the giants all took several steps back.

The key is to loosen up, he thought. Relax your muscles, let the strike drive you back and then . . .

The second strike hit him like a thunderbolt, as the shield edge was slammed into his shoulder. He let out a cry of pain as the blow drove him back. At first, he thought he might actually leave the ground, but he

soon felt the spray of sand at his heels and was able to dig in the shield with renewed strength, gritting his teeth and spitting out a mouthful of saliva with the effort.

All around him, slaves were standing their ground: it had been a good showing for the boys, many of whom seemed to have formed the same strategy of using their shields as breakers. From what he could make out, only five had fallen. He glanced around him, quickly spotting Argon and Olu . . . but not Ruma.

As the trial-master's servants swept forward once again, Decimus threw down his shield and peered nervously over his shoulder.

Ruma lay on the ground several feet behind the line. Despite his cunning, the boy had evidently failed to apply the strategy that had seen so many of the others through: a second cut had opened in his forehead and he was clearly unconscious.

Decimus glanced back at Olu and Argon, but neither could meet his gaze. Their friend was quickly hauled away, and Mori's voice erupted once again:

'Seventeen slaves have now fallen!' he cried. 'Therefore, it has been decided that one lucky boy will receive a pass for the next round. You may all return to your cells.'

As the slave line staggered toward the smaller portcullis, Slavious Doom and his wraith-like companion disappeared into the great archway without so much as a single glance back.

CHAPTER
III

FIST
OF
FURY

'I'm sick of this place!' Decimus screamed, rampaging across his cell and delivering a powerful kick to the wooden frame that had housed Gladius's hay-sacks.

'Shhh!' Argon urged him, his face pressed against the bars that separated their cells. 'Keep quiet, or they'll—'

'I don't CARE!' Decimus brought his foot down on the frame a second time, forcing a splintering crack from the wood. 'I'm sick of evil trial-masters! I'm sick of losing friends and I'm REALLY sick of this food.' He took a run-up and kicked his soup bowl into the air: it shattered against the cell door and the spoon flew out through the bars.

'That's wasn't too clever,' said Olu. 'You know they probably won't give you another one.'

Decimus ignored the two slaves, dropped on to his own bed and turned to face the wall. He'd arrived at Arena Primus with great determination, but he honestly didn't know how much more he could stand.

Sleep overcame him . . . and the shadows lengthened.

He awoke from a nightmare in which a dark figure in flowing robes was trying to force a dagger between his ribs. He wiped a trace of sweat from his brow, moved one of the hay-sacks beneath him and rolled over, trying to drift off once again.

'Shhhh! Quiet! You'll wake the whole section!'

Decimus raised his head and tried to see through the shadows. In the neighbouring cell, Argon was snoring loudly, but there was movement from the third section.

Decimus rubbed the sleep from his eyes and climbed, spider-like, out of the bed. He crawled across the dusty floor and crouched in the corner in order to give himself a better view of the distant cell.

Olu was kneeling at the barred door, whispering to a small shadow that was bent over a bowl in front of him. Decimus squinted into the darkness, and recognized the familiar shape of Skrag, Jailer Truli's mangy little dog.

Ah, he thought. So that's what Olu has been doing with his soup.

He thought for a moment, then cupped a hand to his mouth. 'Pssst!'

Olu almost fell as he spun around, toppling the bowl in the process. The dog shrank back into the shadows, then turned and trotted off along the corridor.

'Who's there?' Olu whispered back. 'Argon?'

'He's asleep. It's me: Decimus.'

'You scared him away!'

'So? You're crazy, Olu! You should be

eating that soup, yourself!'

'He likes it! Besides, that jailer is really cruel to him – the poor little thing is starving to death!'

In the darkness, Decimus rolled his eyes. 'And? Better him than us, I say.'

Olu moved back to his bed. 'Yeah, well – that's your opinion ... and I didn't ask for it. Just go back to sleep, will you?'

Decimus watched the slave settle down, and returned to his own bed.

The following morning, Olu didn't seem to want to speak to either Decimus or Argon, and he quickly moved along the line when the cell doors were opened.

Trial-master Hrin was waiting for the fifteen slaves in the middle of the arena. His fellow masters were watching from the stalls, but there was no sign of Slavious Doom or Drin Hain at the dark arch.

Hrin stepped forward, holding a sack, and raised it above his head.

'Inside this sack,' he yelled, 'are fifteen coloured balls. There are two reds, two blacks, two greens, two yellows, two blues, two browns, two oranges and one white. The slave who draws the white ball will immediately be allowed to return to the cells, and will not need to compete in the trials until tomorrow. Those that draw balls of another colour will face each other in combat, red against red, green against green and so on. The rules of the combat will then be explained. Form up, now!'

As the slaves positioned themselves in a rough line, Hrin walked up to the first boy and held out the sack. A green ball was drawn, and the gangly trial-master moved on.

Decimus watched the proceedings with a detached amusement. It almost felt to him as if he didn't care any more: nothing mattered ... things could only get worse, now. There was no way out. Sooner or later, he would be hauled away to the underground prison. Ultimately, he was doomed.

When the white ball was drawn, Decimus was so lost in his own thoughts that he almost missed the event. As it was, the ball caught his eye at the last second, and his gaze settled upon Olu . . . who stepped back from the slave line with a look of astonishment on his face.

'Lucky boy,' said Hrin, loudly.

'You can say that again,' Argon whispered to Decimus, as the trial-master proceeded down the line. More balls were drawn: green, black, yellow, red, brown and orange.

If Decimus had been paying greater attention to the proceedings, he might not have been quite so surprised when Hrin stopped before him and tossed the sack away.

'There are only red balls remaining,' he muttered. 'You two will fight each other.'

Decimus slowly turned his head . . . and

looked into Argon's determined face. The
Gaul took a breath and stuck out his chin.

'I hope you're ready to lose,' he said.

Decimus shrugged; he was ready.

As Olu was escorted back to the cells,
fourteen slaves paired up and strode out into
the gaping mouth of the arena.

'You will be unarmed for this combat,'
Hrin screamed behind them. 'You may use
fists only. No kicks or grapples are
permitted. The object of the trial is to knock
out your opponent. The victors will progress
into the last eight ... and will move to Arena
Secondus in order to face Grand Master

Doom's public trials. The losers will be imprisoned here, like so many who have fallen before them.'

Decimus glanced at Argon as they walked, but the Gaul was staring straight ahead and marching as if to his day of judgement.

When the pair had reached a suitable distance from all the other combatants, Hrin cried out and the trial began.

Decimus and Argon circled each other.

'You cannot beat me,' Argon snapped, his voice cold. It was almost as if the two had never met, and certainly betrayed no hint of friendship. 'I've watched you in the trials: you're not strong enough or agile enough to take me.'

Decimus said nothing; he simply

continued to circle the Gaul. Neither slave could remove his gaze from the other.

'You're weak, Decimus,' Argon continued. 'Ruma was smarter, Gladius was stronger, Olu and Teo were both quicker. I'm better than you in every way.'

Decimus could feel his anger building, but he knew deep down that the Gaul was speaking the truth.

'Your biggest weakness is that you consider EVERYONE you meet a friend . . . even those who couldn't care less whether you live or die. You pretend to be cold and hard . . . but you are the softest slave here – it really is no wonder your family racked up such debt if you—'

Decimus exploded with rage. Roaring a

battle cry, he thundered over the sand and threw a punch with all his strength behind it.

Then, two very surprising things happened.

First, Argon's lips split into a resigned and happy smile. Then, the Gaul dropped his defence, letting both arms fall to his sides.

Decimus tried to veer off at the last second, but there was too much weight behind the blow. His fist connected with Argon's chin, and the slave collapsed on to the sand.

CHAPTER IV

WOOD AND IRON

Decimus walked back to his cell in silence, a blank look in his eyes as Truli shoved him through the doorway and locked the barred portal behind him.

Olu was sitting on his own bed in the third cell. The boy watched Decimus carefully as he moved over to the far wall and just stood there.

'What happened?' Olu prompted, rising to his feet. 'Where is Argon? Did he get beaten?'

Decimus said nothing.

'What happened to Argon? Is he out?' Olu asked.

Decimus finally turned his head, and two tired, tearful eyes regarded the inquisitive slave.

'He just stood there and let me hit him,' he

said, his hands still shaking. 'He provoked me, going on and on about how weak I was . . . and then he just dropped his guard and stood there.'

'You put Argon out of the trials!' Olu exclaimed.

'No,' said Decimus, sharply. 'ARGON put Argon out of the trials. He could have taken me down at any time. He *chose* to let me hit him.'

'B-but why would he do that?'

Decimus shrugged. 'You tell me. Maybe he'd just given up; maybe he thought he'd get to see the others again if he lost the trials. I just don't know: the only thing I do know is that I want to get out of here . . . more than anything else in the world.'

He collapsed on to his bed, put his head in

his hands and began to sob.

That night, Decimus refused his soup. Olu eagerly claimed his own bowl but, as usual, ate very little.

'Pssst. Wake up.'

The call was soft and low, and barely audible even in the cell from which it had been made.

'Decimus! Psst! Decimus! Wake up!'

Decimus rolled over and continued to snore.

'Decimus Rex! Wake up, or the gods can have you!'

'Mmfhat?'

Decimus sat bolt upright and stared blearily around him. The cell swam in and out of focus as the remains of a good dream drifted away.

'Shhh! Don't speak! It's Olu – can you hear me if I talk like this?'

Decimus licked his dry lips and stifled a cough.

'I can hear you,' he managed. 'Just about.'

'Good.'

Olu crept over to the barred wall between his cell and the one that belonged to Argon and Teo.

Decimus climbed out of bed and tiptoed across to the edge of his own cell.

'What time is it?' he asked, still trying to fight past a painful dryness in his throat.

'Around midnight, I think,' Olu hazarded.

'Right. What do you want? We should be getting some sleep – we're on public trials tomorrow ...'

'You want to go back to sleep? Oh – I thought you wanted to get out of here more than anything else in the world?'

'Of course I do, but—' he froze. 'Why? Do you know of a way out?'

Olu grinned in the darkness.

'No,' he said. 'But you might.'

'Me?' said Decimus. 'I don't understand what you mean?'

'Did you split the wood?'

'What?'

'The other night when you flew into a rage and kicked Gladius's bed all those times: did you actually split the wood?'

Decimus crouched down beside his old friend's bed, removed one of the hay-sacks and felt around the frame.

'Yes,' he said, in conclusion. 'Not completely, but it would come away if I pulled it.'

Decimus tugged at the wood, and there was a soft crack as a length came away in his hand. He held up the piece to show Olu.

'That might be enough,' said the slave, eagerly. 'Throw it to me!'

Decimus crawled back to the bars, reached through and cast the wooden slat towards Olu, who caught it. As he looked on, the scrawny slave hurried over to the front of his cell and began to reach out with the wood, prompting a sudden realization from Decimus.

'Are you trying for Truli's keys?' he whispered.

'Yes. My arms are long, but not quite long enough. I was hoping that … with some extra help … I might be … able …. to—'

Decimus looked on, his mouth gaping in astonishment, as Olu lifted the jailer's keys from their ring.

'Be careful,' he whispered, as the keys gave a tiny jingle. 'The piece on the end is *very* thin.'

Olu nodded, slowly withdrawing his arm. However, just as he was about to step

back, a slamming door somewhere at the end of the corridor caused him to start ... and the keys flew off and clattered to the floor.

For a few seconds, both prisoners froze, praying that their silence would be echoed along the corridor. Fortunately, despite the clatter of the keys, nothing stirred.

'Can you get them?' Decimus whispered.

Olu dropped on to his belly and reached out with the wood: Decimus could almost hear his muscles straining. Eventually, he gave up and raised himself on to his knees.

'They're too far away now,' he said, shaking his head.

Decimus thumped his fist against his leg.

'Damn it!' He hung his head in despair.

'We were SO close. Now what are we going to do? When Truli finds those keys in the morning, he'll—'

'Shhhhh!' Olu put a finger to his lips. 'Just wait! We're not out of the game, yet – my visitor should arrive any second n—'

Skrag trotted out of the shadows, his claws tip-tapping on the stones. The little dog padded over to Olu's cell door and sat down, his head bowed and his eyes turned hopefully upward.

Olu reached under a hay-sack and his arm came out holding the soup bowl. This time, however, he paused before the door, holding the bowl just beyond the little dog's reach.

'Get the keys, Skraggy,' he whispered,

using his other arm to point at the iron ring in the middle of the corridor. 'You see those, boy? Do you?'

Skrag moved his head slightly, but his attention quickly returned to the soup bowl.

'Over here, Skraggy!' Decimus whispered. He had crept across to the front of his own cell and was now reaching an arm through the bars to point at the ring from a second angle. 'See them, boy? Can you get them?'

Skrag was surprised by the second voice, and quickly trotted up to investigate Decimus in case he had his own bowl to offer. On the way, the dog stopped briefly to sniff the key-ring, but quickly dismissed it in favour of the talking figure now crouching in the final cell.

Olu continued to call softly, urging Skrag to make a second detour for the keys. In order to illustrate his point, he had reached out again with the wood.

Skrag looked from the edge of the stick to Olu, and back.

'You KNOW what we want, don't you, Skraggy?' said the slave, holding out the bowl with his other hand. 'If you want THIS, all you have to do is bring them! Bring them, boy – come on!'

'Go on, boy! Please! Get them for us! You can do it! Good boy! Clever Skraggy!' said Decimus.

The little dog hesitated once again, then

reached down and carefully fastened his jaws around the iron ring.

'Good boy!' Decimus called, almost raising his voice in the excitement. 'Goooood boy!'

'Here, Skraggy!' said Olu. He put the bowl on the floor beside the bars. 'Here's your soup, you good dog!'

Skrag trotted over to claim his reward, dropping the keys in the process. They weren't near enough for Olu to reach, but he used the wooden slat to snare them, dragging the iron ring over the stones and snatching it through the bars.

Decimus was shaking with anticipation.

'Do you know which one it is?' he whispered, as Olu rifled through the keys.

The slave nodded. 'I've been watching very closely,' he said, flashing the hyena grin once again. 'You boys talk, Ruma listened, and I watch ...'

CHAPTER V

THE SEARCH

Decimus and Olu crept along the moonlit corridor, keeping their backs to the far wall as they progressed past rows of empty cells and a few that still contained the surviving slaves.

Once they reached the end of the corridor, Olu made to turn left toward the arena, but Decimus grabbed hold of his arm.

'Not that way,' he whispered. 'That tunnel leads to the arena. The other must lead up to the stalls.'

'But we need to get out into the arena!' said Olu, impatiently. 'We can escape through the north portcullis!'

'And wake half the guards in the process?' Decimus shook his head. 'We wouldn't get more than a mile away with Doom's servants bearing down on us – our only hope is to find another way out and do it quietly. If we can sneak out under their noses, we'll be in Calabria by the time Truli makes his breakfast run.'

Olu nodded, and the pair began to move along the corridor.

At length, they came to a set of stone steps that led upward. A sliver of moonlight played over the top flight, and the two slaves took the steps three at a time.

They emerged through an archway that led on to the stalls, and it only took Decimus a second to realize that it was the very same arch through which Slavious Doom and Drin Hain had appeared before the trial of hammers.

A black sky yawned overhead and, if anything, the arena appeared even vaster in moonlight than it had in the bright morning sun. To the fearful slaves, every shadow contained a watchful guard, and every noise was the jailer awaking to check on his prisoners.

Decimus and Olu sped along the stalls, stopping at each intersection in order to race up a new set of steps. Eventually, they reached the highest circle ... and yet another staircase that disappeared into the dark.

'It leads to the roof,' said Decimus, visibly deflating. 'It must do. There is no other way out.'

He hurried after Olu as the quiet slave

reached the top of the new staircase: the pair emerged on to the outer wall of the arena. Nearing the edge, Decimus peered over and studied the distant road below. Olu noticed that the shadow of another great arena loomed in the distance.

'It's too far,' said Decimus, heaving a sigh of despair. 'If we only had a rope or something . . .'

Olu thought for a moment.

'There is *something* we could use,' he said, as Decimus turned to stare at him. 'You remember the ring Hrin dropped on the sand during the combat trials?'

'Yes!' Decimus snapped. 'I remember it because it was full of spikes! We can't use—'

'They didn't run all the way along,' Olu

interrupted. 'There were gaps; hand-sized gaps between each two.'

'How do you *know* that?'

Olu shrugged. 'As I said before, I watch things carefully . . . I pay attention to detail.'

'That's obvious – but how in the name of the gods are we going to find it?'

'It can't be difficult,' said Olu. 'It has to be in the arena, somewhere . . . possibly in a supply room, though Ruma would probably have heard if such a place existed. It's more likely that it's kept in Hrin's quarters . . .'

'Right,' Decimus nodded. 'But so is Hrin . . . and I really don't want to go sneaking around in a room where a trial-master is sleeping.'

Olu smiled nervously. 'Do you think we have a choice?' he said.

The handle turned, and the door creaked
open on tired hinges. When it was just large
enough to accommodate a head, one appeared
through the gap.

'Any luck?' Decimus whispered.

Olu withdrew from the doorway and
quietly closed the door behind him.

'It's Mori's room,' he explained, speaking
so silently that he was almost mouthing the
words. 'Shall we go in?'

Decimus shook his head. 'We could
search through all of them, but I really don't
want to do that unless we draw a blank with
Hrin – the combat trials are his, after all.'

'The room seemed pretty bare, anyway. If there was a massive spiked chain in there, I'd have seen it. Let's move on.'

The next three doors revealed two separate servant quarters and the private chamber belonging to ageing trial-master Falni. There was no sign of Hrin or the chain.

'This is insane!' Decimus whispered, when they arrived back at the intersection with the arena and the main cell corridor. 'We've checked every room! In the name of the gods, where IS he?'

'Maybe he doesn't live here like the others. It's pretty obvious that Slavious Doom and his weird friend don't!'

Decimus thought for a moment. 'You could be right,' he said. 'He always seemed to

be dressed a bit grander than Mori and Falni
... and his breastplate looked a lot more
expensive. Maybe he was the chief trial-
master? He's probably got a house in town or
something! This is a nightmare!'

'Shhh!' Olu waved down his companion.
'What about that other door – the one back
in the prison block?'

'That's Truli's chamber,' said Decimus,
sarcastically. 'I doubt Hrin sleeps in there.'

'Maybe not, but it's the only room we
haven't tried so what have we got to lose? It's
either that or the portcullis . . .'

'Fine, let's go . . . *quietly*.'

The two slaves retraced their steps and
crept along the cell corridor, amid the distant
sounds of snoring and groaning wood.

Decimus put his hand on the door handle and slowly turned it clockwise. Fortunately, the door didn't creak as it was opened.

Truli was sprawled on a makeshift bed that wasn't greatly different from the ones in the cells. The jailer's massive stomach looked like a small mountain rising and falling in the shadowy room. The chamber itself was immense; at least twice the size of the others they had seen. One wall was stacked with the wooden platforms that had claimed Gladius and the floor next to it was piled with the long poles that had supported them. At the back of the room was a collection of shields, hammers and, curled in the furthest corner like a giant python, the spiked chain from Hrin's combat trials.

Decimus froze when he saw it, and made
a quick and silent gesture to Olu, who tried
to sneak past him but found his way barred.

'No,' he whispered. 'Let me go: you
watch the corridor.'

Olu nodded, and looked on nervously as

Decimus sneaked deeper into the room. There was a brief moment of concern when Truli stopped snoring abruptly, but the danger soon passed and the hulking brute rolled on to his side.

Decimus moved over to the far wall and began to creep toward the corner. When he arrived beside the spiked chain, he crouched down and tried to lift it ... but the cursed thing weighed a ton.

'Olu!' he called, one eye on the sleeping giant. 'I'm going to need some help.'

The other slave tiptoed into the room, knelt down beside him and carefully took hold of the chain.

'Together,' Decimus muttered, and the pair began to lift the immense chain between them. They got as far as the bed when Truli suddenly rolled over and sat up.

Decimus started, and Olu gasped: they only just managed to hold on to the chain as, to their horror, the immense jailer climbed off his ragged bed and slammed across the floor toward them.

Frozen with fear, the two slaves looked on, powerless, as the ugly giant pulled a heavy-looking sword from a wooden barrel at the end of his bed and advanced on the duo, raising the blade above him to strike them down.

'Move!' Decimus hissed, but Olu was absolutely rooted to the spot with fear.

The sword came down in a direct strike . . . and stopped inches from Olu's head.

The two slaves ducked to avoid the blow, and both of them gasped as the moonlight illuminated Truli's face. The jailer was fast asleep, but he was also preparing for another strike. Whatever enemy he was facing in the dreamlands, he seemed determined to overcome it.

Olu put all his strength into hoisting up his part of the chain. 'Is he—'

'Sleepwalking,' Decimus finished. 'We need to get out of here, before he walks into something solid and wakes up for real.'

They hurried from the room, barely supporting the enormous chain between them – and made for the roof of the arena.

CHAPTER
VI
THE
DESCENT

ecimus hooked the end of the chain around one of several stones that adorned the circular roof of the stadium. He and Olu managed to haul the incredible bulk of the chain over the edge of the arena roof, but neither had considered the noise it might make as it unravelled. The resulting clatter was enough to wake half the surrounding town, let alone the many inhabitants of the arena below.

Sure enough, several torches struck up in the darkness as the two slaves began to descend, pausing carefully between each section to ensure they didn't grab a handful of spikes by mistake. The distant sound of slamming doors signalled that the servants were now aware that something was afoot,

but

three

'Dr

awkwardly, but seemed to be un

'It's not that far, and th

Decimus release

dropped afte

'Th

...nks, then

let go of the chain

and plunged to

the ground. He

landed

harmed.

ground is soft!'

his grip on the link and

his companion.

town,' he said, stumbling as he landed
and quickly bursting into a sprint. 'We need
a place to hide.'

The two friends picked up their pace, and
dashed off in the direction of Avellino.

Several hours later, in a palatial room at the
top of a vast manor on the edge of Amalfi,
two servants admitted trial-master Hrin to a
private audience with Slavious Doom.

As the doors were closed behind him, the

tall master moved into the centre of the room and bowed low. He did not raise his head as he started to speak.

'My lord,' he began. 'I have grave news to report.'

Slavious Doom, resplendent on a golden throne, didn't bother to rise in response to the statement. Instead, he yawned a little, removed the golden helm that adorned his head and focused his eyes on the trial-master bowing before him.

'Do not raise your head until I give you permission to do so,' he said.

Hrin said nothing. He maintained his position perfectly, his ragged breath alone betraying him as a living creature.

Doom blinked only once. 'Continue.'

'Two slaves have escaped Arena Primus,' said the bowed master.

'I see. How, exactly?'

'Well, my lord, they . . . stole a spiked chain from the jailer's quarters – one used in the trials we set them – and—'

'How clever.' Doom's voice was silky; almost snake-like. His lips split in a sickly smile. 'It is no great surprise that a slave would escape eventually . . . even two. They must be incredibly resourceful.' He leaned forward on the throne. 'You will find them, of course?'

'Of course, my lord.' Hrin paused; he was beginning to shake slightly. 'But . . .'

'There is something else?'

'Yes, my lord. One of the escapees is a boy

called Olu. The other is . . . that is . . . he—'

'Well?'

'He is the boy you personally requested us to find, my lord: the one who the scriptures say will . . . retrieve The Sword.'

'Decimus Rex,' said Doom, slowly rising from his throne. The grand master drew a stout blade from a silver box beside him and, very slowly, progressed down the half-dozen steps that separated the gleaming dais from the floor. 'Decimus Rex . . . is . . . gone?'

'Yes, my lord,' Hrin confirmed, a bead of sweat forming on his brow as he finally dared to raise his head. 'If I may remind Your Excellency, Master Mori and I did suggest he be quartered separately but you-you-you did specifically request he should be treated like all the oth—'

Hrin froze, his eyes wide and his smile a sinister mask.

For the briefest of seconds, nothing happened.

Then the trial-master's gaunt head slipped from his shoulders and rolled across the marble floor. The body collapsed after it.

Slavious Doom looked down at his handiwork, and smiled. When he turned back to face his throne, a dark figure had detached itself from the shadows behind the dais and was standing mere feet away. It moved like a ghost, and was dressed from head to toe in a flowing black cloak.

'Decimus Rex has escaped us, Drin,' Doom growled, every hint of pleasantry

draining from his voice. 'He is in the
company of a fellow slave. Find him, and
bring him back – at all costs.' He ascended
the dais and replaced his sword inside the
silver box. 'You may kill the other one,'
he muttered.

OUT NOW

When Decimus Rex and his friend Olu escape the dreaded Arena Primus, overlord Slavious Doom is furious and demands their immediate capture. A frantic and determined search follows. From the wild dogs running riot in the sewers, to the soldiers scouring the towns above, it seems only a matter of time before they are caught. Can the pair evade Doom's dreaded servant, Drin Hain? Find out now in . . .

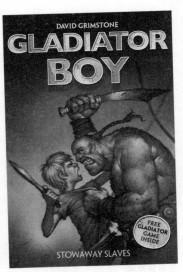

STOWAWAY SLAVES

ARENA COMBAT

Get ready to challenge your friends! Each Gladiator Boy book will contain a different trial – collect them all to run your own Arena of Doom – either at home or in the school playground.

TRIAL 2
HAMMER AND SHIELD!

You will need three players – an attacker, a defender and a referee. This game is easy to play, but difficult to win! The attacking player decides whether he will strike from the left, the right or straight ahead and indicates by raising either his left fist, his right fist or both fists together (as a straight attack). The defending player must close his eyes and announce whether he is blocking left, right or centre. If he shouts 'left' and the strike was to the left, he has blocked it! Otherwise, he takes a 'hit'. The attack then passes to the opponent and the game continues.

Here are the hand signs:

LEFT OF THE PERSON

The first player to win 3 games out of 5 is declared the winner!

You can either play the game as yourselves or, when you have collected all the Decimus Rex books, you can take on the roles of the gladiatorial slaves and use their special character profiles to fire your imagination!

RIGHT OF THE PERSON

TWO FISTS AHEAD

CHARACTER PROFILE
ARGON

NAME: Argon

FROM: Gaul

HEIGHT: 1.75 metres

BODY TYPE: Muscular

BEST FRIEND: Olu

CELLMATE: Teo

ARGON QUIZ: How well do you know Argon? Can you answer the following three questions?

1. ARGON IS THE FIRST PERSON TO SPOT THE JAILER'S KEYS. TRUE OR FALSE?

2. WHAT TRIAL DOES ARGON DESCRIBE AS 'BAD, REALLY BAD'?

3. WHO DOES ARGON TELL TO 'KEEP QUIET' FOR FEAR OF BEING OVERHEARD?

Answers: 1. True **2.** Platform trial, page 26 **3.** Decimus, page 48

WEAPON PROFILE THE HAMMER

The hammer has always been used as a tool for making an impact on a difficult surface or for driving in a nail. However, it was once used as a weapon and known variously as 'great-hammer' or 'war-hammer'.

There are few versions of the weapon as the design was so simple. However, the handles of these hammers made them different from each other. Handles tended to be either long (great-hammer) or short (war-hammer). The hammers used in Gladiator Boy are great-hammers.

A WAR-HAMMER

A war-hammer can be used with a shield, as it requires only one hand

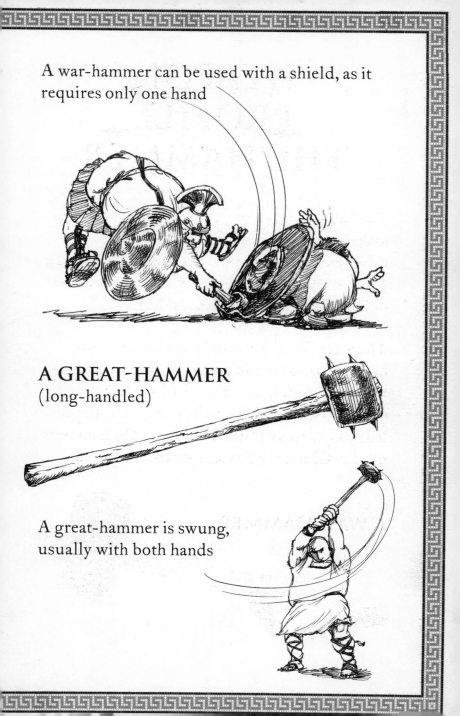

A GREAT-HAMMER
(long-handled)

A great-hammer is swung, usually with both hands

GLADIATOR BOY

Check out the Gladiator Boy website for games, downloads, activities, sneak previews and lots of fun! You can even get extra pieces of the arena and fantastic action figures! Sign up to the newsletter to receive exclusive extra content and the opportunity to enter special competitions.

WWW.GLADIATORBOY.COM

LET BATTLE COMMENCE!

MAKE YOUR OWN ARENA OF DOOM

1. Carefully cut around the outline of the arena section. Ask an adult to help if necessary.
2. Fold across line A. Use a ruler to get a straight edge.
3. Fold across line B. Use a ruler to get a straight edge.
4. Ask an adult to help you score along lines C & D with a pair of sharp scissors.
5. Fold up over line E and push the window out.
6. Repeat instructions 1 to 5 for every Arena of Doom piece collected.
7. Glue the top of each tab and stick them to the next piece of the arena. Repeat as necessary.

CHECK OUT THE WEBSITE FOR A PHOTO OF THE COMPLETE ARENA.

TO MAKE YOUR ACTION FIGURE

1. Cut around the outline of the figure. Ask an adult to help if necessary.
2. Cut along slot X at the bottom of the figure.
3. Cut out Gladiator Boy rectangle.
4. Cut along slot Y.
5. Slot figure into slot Y.

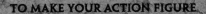